FUNNYBONES

Other books by Allan Ahlberg

A BIT MORE BERT

THE ADVENTURES OF BERT

The FAST FOX, SLOW DOG series (illus. André Amstutz)

FUNNYBONES: THE BLACK CAT (illus. André Amstutz)

FUNNYBONES: BUMPS IN THE NIGHT (illus. André Amstutz)

FUNNYBONES: DINOSAUR DREAMS (illus. André Amstutz)

FUNNYBONES: GIVE THE DOG A BONE (illus. André Amstutz)

FUNNYBONES: MYSTERY TOUR (illus. André Amstutz)

FUNNYBONES: THE PET SHOP (illus. André Amstutz)

FUNNYBONES: THE SKELETON CREW (illus. André Amstutz)

The HAPPY FAMILIES series (illus. various)

THE LITTLE CAT BABY

Other books by Janet and Allan Ahlberg

THE BABY'S CATALOGUE

BURGLAR BILL

BYE BYE BABY

THE CLOTHES HORSE AND OTHER STORIES

COPS AND ROBBERS

EACH PEACH PEAR PLUM

FUNNYBONES

IT WAS A DARK AND STORMY NIGHT

JEREMIAH IN THE DARK WOODS

THE JOLLY CHRISTMAS POSTMAN

THE JOLLY POSTMAN

THE JOLLY POCKET POSTMAN

PEEPO!

STARTING SCHOOL

Mystery Tour

ALLAN AHLBERG • ANDRÉ AMSTUTZ

PUFFIN

In a dark dark town,
down a dark dark street,
in a dark dark car,
at a red red traffic light

. . . . three skeletons are waiting.

"What shall we do tonight?"
says the big skeleton.
"Let's go on a mystery tour,"
the little skeleton says.
"Good idea!" says the big skeleton.
"What's a mystery tour?"
"I can't tell you,"
the little skeleton says.
"It's a mystery!"

Then the red red traffic light
turns green
. . . and the mystery tour begins.

The dark dark car drives
down the dark dark street
to mystery number one.

"What's that?" says the little skeleton.
"I know," the big skeleton says,
"it's a . . .

. . . baby in a cot!"

The dark dark car drives
down the dark dark street,
round the dark dark corner
to mystery number two.

"What's that?" says the big skeleton.
"I know," the little skeleton says,
"it's a . . .

". . . teddy in a tent!"

Two mysteries:
a teddy in a tent
and a baby in a cot.

The dark dark car drives
down the dark dark street,
past the dark dark park
and the dark dark zoo
to mystery number three.

"I know," says the big skeleton,
"it's a . . .

NUMBER 3

. . . black cat on a roof!"

And mystery number four.
"It's a bag of bones,"
the little skeleton says.
"No, it's not," says the big skeleton.
"If we put them all together, it's a . . .

. . . parrot!"

"Thanks very much!" says the parrot,
and she flies away.

The dark dark car drives
down the dark dark street,
up and down the dark dark hill
to mystery number five.

"Whooooo!" goes mystery number five.
And what is it . . .?

. . .A ghost on a train!

Five mysteries:
a ghost on a train,
a bag of bones
(that was really a parrot),
a black cat on a roof,
a teddy in a tent
and a baby in a cot.

The dark dark car drives
down the dark dark street,
round the dark dark corner,
past the dark dark park
and the dark dark zoo,
up and down the dark dark hill,
in and out of the dark dark petrol station
to mystery number six.

TO MYSTERY NUMBER 6

"I know what mystery number six is," says the little skeleton.
"Me, too!" the big skeleton says, "it's . . .

Now the mystery tour is ended . . .
well, nearly.
There's just one more mystery.
"What's that?" says the little skeleton.
"Where's the car?"
the big skeleton says.

Where's the car?

A dark dark car
in a dark dark car-park
is hard to find.

P

EXIT

The End

PUFFIN BOOKS

Published by the Penguin Group: London, New York, Ireland, Australia, Canada, India, New Zealand and South Africa

Penguin Books Ltd, Registered Offices: 80 Strand, London WC2R 0RL, England

puffinbooks.com

First published by William Heinemann Ltd 1991
First published in Puffin Books 2006
007